Brave As

JANICE MARRIOTT

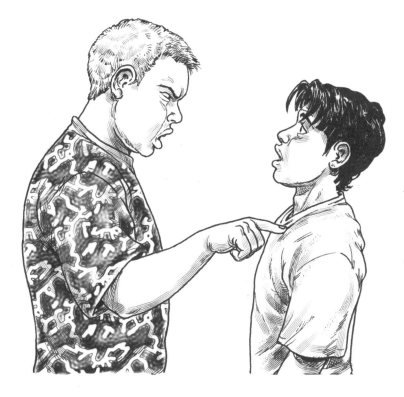

illustrated by Gus Hunter

Learning Media

Chapter 1

"I– I don't want my hair c-cut!"

"That's tough. I've made the appointment for after school." Mom's like that. When she's in a hurry, she doesn't seem to care. "You're meeting Wayne at dinner, remember? You have to look smart."

"I-I don't want to meet W-Wayne."

"Tough. You have to look smart and be brave."

That was mean. Mom wasn't usually like that. But since she met Wayne, she doesn't seem to care so much about what she says to me. Wayne is this guy Mom went out with a couple of times last week. It must be a big deal for her because she'll only let me meet him when I've come straight from a haircut. "Move it!" she shouted from the doorway. "I don't want to be late. I've got a banquet to prepare."

I slouched out into the early morning sunshine with my huge backpack. "I-I've f-forgotten my speech!" I dashed back inside for my folder. It was by my bed, where I'd been trying to say my speech last night. Today was the school day I was most dreading in my whole life. The worst day on earth since the dinosaurs got exterminated. Today I had to give a speech in front of the whole class.

The phone rang. It was Jules from school. He wanted to borrow Mom's salad dryer. "What? You into c-c-cooking?" I asked.

"Just bring it," he snapped. "Meet you in the locker room. Go!"

Mom's a cook. That's how she makes her living. We have all the gadgets. Mom got the salad dryer out of the cupboard. She quickly tied on a label with my name on it. "I want it back," she said.

She showed me how it worked. You put the lettuce or whatever into a wire basket with handles. Then you closed the top and whirled it round and round, and the water shot out. "Outside," said Mom, swinging the car keys.

"I know you use it outside," I said.

"No, I mean *you*, outside! I'm late!"

Had the world gone mad? Why did Jules want to make salad? And why ask me? I had never ever been his friend.

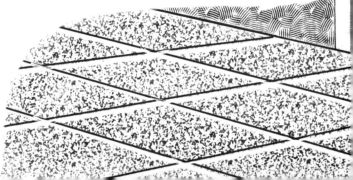

Chapter 2

The first bad thing happened outside our front door. Mom kissed me!

I walked away quickly, hoping no one had seen. I looked up. Sarah Bernstein was coming down the road, surrounded by giggling girlfriends as usual. And she was looking straight at me with those two sharp green eyes of hers. Sarah Bernstein had seen. That's what I get for living right across the road from school.

"Good luck with your speech!" That was Mom, bellowing out the car window and then revving the motor far too loudly and roaring off down the road.

Sarah Bernstein heard. She must have heard. I wished a huge excavator were coming down the road with its jaws open and I could hop in and be crushed to bits. Instead, Sarah kept looking and listening. She kept coming down the road, surrounded by all those other kids.

Sarah is never ever alone. She is the most popular girl in the school. She never speaks to me. I stared at her. I saw her perfect pink lips open. I saw a glint of white, shiny teeth. The lips drew back slowly. She smiled. A real smile with two rows of gleaming teeth and glittering eyes.

"Hi, Matt," she said. *She* said. This could not be happening. I must have flipped into a different universe. I couldn't speak. I was completely paralyzed. Even my toenails stopped growing.

I froze. I stared. I must have looked like a snowman with two lumps of coal for eyes and a carrot for a nose.

Sarah came closer and closer until she was right beside me. I thought of things I could say, like "Hi!" or "How ya doin'?" But no words came out at all. My tongue and my brain weren't connected. Then it was too late. She'd gone. Sarah had passed by. I flipped back into this universe. Nothing *that* bad could happen for the rest of the day.

I looked down at my hands. I was carrying the salad basket. It was just hanging there, in front of me – a stupid wire basket with handles. Sarah must have seen it. And why did I have it anyway? Then I remembered: I had to give it to Jules. Hmm … maybe something else bad *was* about to happen.

Chapter 3

I rushed to the locker room and handed over the salad dryer. I tried to make a run for it, but nothing's that easy, is it? I couldn't get away. Jules hung onto the salad dryer, and he hung onto me. His arm was twisted in the back of my T-shirt.

Jules said he was recruiting members for his new DSB gang.

"W-w-what's that?" I managed to say.

"Do Something Brave, Dumbo."

If it was Do Something Brave, Dumbo, it'd be DSBD. I thought that, but I didn't dare say it. I'm like that. I think stuff, but my brain isn't hard-wired to my tongue. My thoughts don't come out as words. They come out as pictures that only I can see.

It was just as well I didn't say anything to Jules. He wouldn't have liked it. And I was scared of Jules. He was known as a guy who carried out any threats he made.

"Nah. We don't want you in DSB." He stood over me. He seemed huge – bigger than me in every way. You could have wrapped me up with him, like scraps in a sheet of newspaper. "Cause you're a scaredy cat."

I opened my mouth. No words came out.

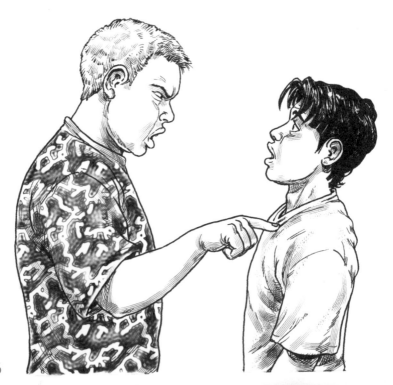

"What do you mean by something brave?"
Malcolm asked. Malcolm was bigger than Jules if
you put them back to back.

"Something brave like disconnecting the school
computers, exploding a river mud bomb ..."

"Why?"

"To show you're brave."

"Wow!"

"I dare you. I just dare you!" shouted Jules.

"Mud everywhere!" He swung round with the salad dryer in both his hands. Now I knew what the dryer was for.

"I'd do that," said Richard.

Malcolm and I stepped back a bit so that we could look at Richard.

"Would you now?" asked Jules.

"I reckon."

Malcolm and I didn't move.

"At lunchtime?"

"Why not."

"In the staff room?"

We all jumped. In the staff room! Jules had to be crazy.

"Aw, maybe not, eh?" Richard backed down.

"OK, then. I'll do it myself," said Jules. "I'll show you who's brave." He stared at each of us in turn. "And if the teachers find out, I'll know who told, won't I?" He stared real hard at me. His eyeballs wobbled. Then he ran off.

Chapter 4

$\mathcal{I}$ forgot about Jules and his gang. All morning I worried about my speech. I was going to have to stand in front of the whole class and talk. Me! I felt like I was going to throw up any minute. From nerves. I didn't dare go up to Mrs. Kemp and tell her. A chicken came onto the picture screen in my head. A chicken? Yeah! A chicken, with my face.

"You OK, Matt?" Mrs. Kemp was beside my desk with her head on one side. She looked like a chicken too. I was freaking out.

"Perhaps you'd like to go up to the office and tell Mrs. Scott to save me some lunch. I think there's Sloppy Joe on the menu."

That did it. I ran out of the classroom fast and threw up round the back of Block 3. Unfortunately Mr. Rodriguez, the caretaker, was passing with his dog. That was the third bad thing that had happened to me that day.

Mr. Rodriguez took me up to the office to see if he could find anyone there who'd know what to do with me. Mrs. Scott told me to lie down on the window seat in the staff room. "Nice and sunny there. Lovely day. Everyone's outside."

I lay there with my eyes tightly shut. I could hear all the kids playing. They didn't have any worries about speeches. Some teachers were sitting outside on benches. They were chatting and drinking coffee. No one was worried about making a silly speech about kites. No one except me. No one was stuck inside, in the staff room. No one except me.

Then I heard a noise. A "door creaking open" noise. I heard a click. A "door clicking shut" kind of click. I heard a couple of slow, carefully placed footsteps. I opened my aching eyes.

Chapter 5

Jules was standing there with a paper sack wobbling in his hand. It was wobbling because it was full of river mud. "Don't move," he hissed, "or you're history!" He laid the wobbly sack on the table and carefully took my salad dryer out of his backpack, the salad dryer with *my* name dangling from it.

I'd be history if I got up and screamed. I'd be history if I stayed there lying on the window seat. It's times like this you know whether you're brave or not. I'm not. I shut my eyes again. I looked at my built-in picture screen and saw Sarah, chickens, the hairdresser, Mom swinging her car keys, my speech folder …. I decided that I was an unlucky person living a very unlucky life.

I didn't open my eyes, but I could hear Jules putting the mud into the salad dryer and then pouring water into the mud. I heard him spinning round and round. I heard splatter noises. I *felt* mud splatter all over me. Then I heard heavy breathing.

"That's fixed you," Jules said. "Chicken."

I heard the door click open and shut. I opened my eyes, and … the fourth bad thing was happening.

Mud dripped from the ceiling, the walls, the lamps, the bulletin boards, the bookshelves. Mud dripped from my hair. I sat up. Mud dripped down the back of my neck. Why would anyone want to do that? Jules must be psycho.

I got up and stood there like a statue. Not only did I have no words – this time I had nothing on my picture screen either. I was stunned. My body and mind were unplugged, switched off, gone. Then my ears came alive. I heard the door open.

Chapter 6

It wasn't Mrs. Kemp coming in to see how I was. It was Mr. Grock, the principal. I always knew I was unlucky. Now I had proof.

He stared at me, at the walls, at the mud. He stared at the salad dryer Jules had left on the table. He stared at the label hanging from it.

Mr. Grock's face swelled up. His eyes seemed to stand out from his face. He looked like he was changing into a large toad.

His mouth opened and shut, opened and shut. No sound. No words. A tide of red flooded his skin. He opened his mouth once more. Giant creases appeared alongside his mouth, from his nose to his chin. More creases cracked across his forehead. I thought he was going to burst.

"What? What?" The words roared out of him like rocket fuel. He could launch himself up through the ceiling now with that power. Maybe he would. Maybe he'd whizz round the stars and burn up on re-entry. My mind and its picture screen had started working again.

Mrs. Kemp appeared behind his shoulder. She looked at the mud-splattered floor, walls, and ceiling and the mud dripping slowly from the bottom of the light bulbs. She looked at me. "Matt, get into the staff bathroom and clean yourself up." She turned to Mr. Grock. "Lock this door. No one's allowed in here," she said. Mrs. Kemp's brain was never disconnected from her tongue. Never.

From the bathroom, I could hear Mr. Grock shouting even before I'd cleaned the mud from my ears. First they thought I did it. Then they thought I must know who did it. If I squealed on Jules, he'd stuff me into my backpack with a couple of huge stones and throw it, and me, of course, into the river. I didn't dare tell on him. I wasn't brave enough.

They questioned me in Mr. Grock's office while muddy water dripped from my hair onto his carpet. I said I didn't see anyone come in. They said I was lying.

"Why did you do this?" asked Mrs. Kemp. "Was it because of the speech competition?"

"You did do it, didn't you?" screamed Mr. Grock.

"No, I d-d-d-didn't!"

"You'd better go home," said Mrs. Kemp very quietly.

"I can't hear. M-my ears …"

"Go home!" boomed Mr. Grock. "Go home and clean yourself up! Then get back to your class!" His face still looked swollen and red, but it had lost its lift-off energy. "Tell your mother I'll be calling her."

I walked out of the school gate and across the road to our front door, dripping icky, sticky river mud behind me. Five bad things in one day, and it was only lunchtime. But who's counting? Not me anymore. I decided to have a bath.

Chapter 7

Mom wasn't home, of course, but Mr. Grock didn't know that. I didn't know how to clean myself up. Everything I did made the river mud spread onto other things like the carpet, the chairs, and the counter, but none of it seemed to come off me. On my built-in picture screen, I saw the mud spreading through the house, possibly the street, maybe the whole world.

I turned the water on. I peeled off my clothes and climbed into the bath. Then I poured all the bubble bath into the brown water. I lay there, listening to the bubbles popping close to my ears. *It'll-be-all-right. It'll-be-all-right.* By the time I'd filled and emptied the bath three times, I began to feel a bit better.

Then I remembered my speech. I had to do it this afternoon! Everyone in class had to do a speech. Mom and I had talked to Mrs. Kemp ages ago, before speeches became something to worry about. We'd agreed I'd do what everyone else did. I didn't want any special favors.

But giving a speech is my idea of the worst thing that could happen to anyone. It's worse than river mud splattered on your face. It's worse than Mr. Grock thinking you ruined the staff room. It's a horror story, but I had to do it.

I got out of the bath. My teeth were chattering with fright. I left the pile of slimy brown clothes on the floor and dripped clean water into my bedroom, where I put on my favorite clothes – my new jeans and my Michael Jordan T-shirt with "Stand Tall" written across it. Then I dived down into the hidden depths of me and found some courage, and I walked back across the road to school holding the courage in my hands. It felt like that, anyway.

I opened the classroom door.

Chapter

8

The kids were all sitting there listening to Sarah's speech about shopping on the Internet. I sat down and waited. I wanted to hear her speech. It must have been fascinating. Everything about Sarah was fascinating. But all I could hear was my own voice, drumming in my ears like a rock band. Everyone clapped, and Sarah walked back to her seat.

"Very good, Sarah. Ah, we do have Matt with us, after all." Mrs. Kemp was being ultracool. I wasn't sure whether it was because of the river mud or me doing the speech. I got up, carried my speech folder to the front of the whole class, and opened my mouth. "I'm g-g-going to t-t-talk to you today ab-b-b-bout k-k-k-kites."

Someone giggled. It was Jules, sitting there in the front row. I felt the same lift-off anger Mr. Grock must have felt in the staff room. The blood in my ears beat like drums. I stared at Jules, straight into his eyes. He wasn't going to ruin the speech I'd practiced for days and days. No way.

"I-I-I have a bird k-k-k-ite." It was terrible, but I kept going. The drum beats in my ears helped me get the words out on time if I tried to speak on the beat. Most of the kids sat with their heads on their desks and their arms wrapped round them. If anyone looked up, I stared at them hard, the way Jules had stared at me this morning.

"Th-th-thank you for listening to m-m-my speech." It was over! My T-shirt was stuck to me. My hands were sticky with sweat. I collapsed back into my seat.

The school secretary came into the room. "Mrs. Kemp, could Jules go to the principal?" Everyone gasped. I was terrified. I hadn't squealed on Jules, but what if he thought I had?

chapter

9

After school, I was walking along the road to the hairdresser. I was just about to cross the bridge. The sun was sparkling on the river. Mrs. Kemp and Mr. Grock hadn't said anything more to me about the mess. I hadn't been arrested. Jules hadn't drowned me. He hadn't come back to class after seeing Mr. Grock. Malcolm said Jules wouldn't be coming back, ever. The speech was over for a whole year. Life was pretty good.

Suddenly a car steered right up close to me. It stopped. I didn't dare look up. Did he have the stones with him? Would anyone see him and his dad throw me over the railing? How long does it take to drown?

"Want a ride?" It was Sarah. Her mom smiled from the driver's seat. "Have a French fry," Sarah said as I hopped in. Life was getting better and better.

45

"You don't usually go this way."

"Haircut."

"You're brave."

"B-b-b-brave? To g-g-g-get my hair cut?"

"No. To do the speech. I think you're the bravest person I know."

I was speechless.

The hairdresser was a new guy. He called himself a hair designer. "What style are you having?"

"Haven't th-th-th-thought about it."

"Well, how brave are you?"

One and a half hours later, I left the hairdresser with a "high and tight," just like a marine. Except mine was dyed blond.

I strolled off to Mom's work to meet this Wayne character. It didn't worry me at all, meeting him. I was brave enough.